SOME GIRLS BIND

RORY JAMES

An imprint of Enslow Publishing

WEST **44** BOOKS™

Please visit our website, www.west44books.com. For a free color catalog of all our high-quality books, call toll free 1-800-542-2595 or fax 1-877-542-2596.

Cataloging-in-Publication Data

Names: James, Rory.
Title: Some girls bind / Rory James.
Description: New York : West 44, 2019. | Series: West 44 YA verse
Identifiers: ISBN 9781538382530 (pbk.) | ISBN 9781538382547 (library bound) | ISBN 9781538383278 (ebook)
Subjects: LCSH: Children's poetry, American. | Children's poetry, English. | English poetry.
Classification: LCC PS586.3 S664 2019 | DDC 811'.60809282--dc23

First Edition
Published in 2019 by
Enslow Publishing LLC
101 West 23rd Street, Suite #240
New York, NY 10011

Editor: Caitie McAneney
Designer: Sam DeMartin

Printed in the United States of America

CPSIA compliance information: Batch #CS18W44: For further information contact
Enslow Publishing LLC, New York, New York at 1-800-542-2595.

EVERYONE HAS A SECRET IN HIGH SCHOOL

At least, that's what
my older brother, Steve, says.

Some girls date
"bad boys."
Sneak out their windows.
Run off on motorcycles
with dropouts.
("You know," he shrugs.
"Like in the movies.")

Some girls ask:
"Hey Mom, Dad,
can I have some friends
over to watch Disney movies?"
Mickey and Minnie are harmless.
But they always wear gloves.
Maybe it's so they don't
leave fingerprints on
their parents' wine bottles.

Some girls play
spin the bottle,
around and around it goes.
But I don't know.
I've never met anyone
who has actually played.

1

My friends see movies
and eat ice cream.
      And, according to my mother,
      have "teenage" problems.

(Three years
into my teens,
and not even I
know what she
means by this.)

I'm pretty sure
      my parents
      would never believe
      that I was one of
      "those girls."

Would never think
that I have a secret.

      (I'm not, I do).

My friends have secrets too,
but not like the ones
found in the feel-good
section of Netflix:

> Levi's gay.
>> (He and Evan Holmes
>> just started dating.
>> But neither has told his parents.)
>> And

> Nora's dad drinks too much.
>> (She puts her brothers
>> to bed every night.)
>> And

> Eric wants to drop out of swimming.
>> (But doesn't
>> because of scholarships.)
>> And

> I think Jason and Callie
> have secrets too, but
>> we all hang out
>> and don't talk about them.

Instead,
we pile into Eric's van
and drive to the park.

Climb down
onto the rocks
by the canal.
Off of the trails where

our parents
brought us for
Sunday cookouts.
Days with
picture-perfect
picnic baskets and
family Frisbee matches.

We talk about
our classmates and
our teachers.
Complain about
homework, tests,
and quizzes.

We talk about
everything except
the feeling of keeping secrets.
But we do keep them here,
                    in this place.

Levi was the first to share his.

Coming out to us was
    a rite of passage
    scarier than becoming a man.
    Nora rose first to hug him,
    maybe remembering
    the way they danced
    at his bar mitzvah.
    He dropped the rock
    he'd been holding. The one
    he meant to skip.
    We all picked up his secret.

One by one,
we each come
to the canal.

Pick a normal weekend outing.

Hold court.
Call a meeting.
All of those adult terms
we'd heard our
parents talk about.
To say to the water what scared us most.
To watch our reflections
instead of meeting friends' eyes.

We listen for secrets
and we tell our own.

All of us except
for me.

I have one, too. And
I had hoped
it would join
my brother's list of examples.
That I would be a "some girl."

But, of course,
what other teenage girl
binds her chest
because she's not sure
she's a girl?

TIES THAT BIND

I started when I was 14.
     Found a once too-big
     (now too-tight) vest.
     The buttons strained over a
     white undershirt.
     I wrapped tape around
     the shoulders of the vest,
     forming thin straps
     not exactly hidden.

No one could get too close.
     Couldn't run their fingers
     over my back.
     Notice the braless broad shoulders
     covered in the silk of a stretched vest.

Getting dressed each morning,
     I stand behind my door.
          Off to the side. So if it opens,
    I am behind it. Hidden by
the Scooby-Doo blanket I use
as a closet door.
I feel its soft
fleece as
I pull one layer and
         then another over my shoulders.

I remember the first time I wore it,
the first time I felt the ridge
of one button
slide into place and
then the next.

The first time I added
another layer
to my already boyish style
hiding beneath T-shirts.

My parents were
out of town for the day.

I was free.

That day, I'd curled next to my dog,
        toyed with the idea of binding,
        of my body looking more
        like what I expected to see
        in the mirror.
        The idea grew
        and grew. The pages
        left in my summer reading
        lessened. My
        notes of quotes for the paper
        I had to write sat off to the side.

I snuck into my room for no reason.
        Asked my dog to keep this secret
        as he had all others.
        (He did.)

MY PARENTS

My mother already wondered why
       I wore white undershirts every day.
       Gave me a hard time
       when, in the store,
       I'd try to put a set in our cart.
       She'd ask, "Where did you even get this idea?"

I knew that "Dad" was not
       the right answer,
       though it was the truest.
       I watched the line
       between men and me drawn
       in permanent marker on the drive home.
       Watching the white dotted lane lines
       become a solid double yellow.

 I soon used money from my job at the library
        to buy undershirts by myself so Mom wouldn't see.

The vest on my chest would be her shame.
       The binder,
       a binding family secret. So
       I say nothing, hide everything.

I barely know how to explain it to myself.
        That it's like a corset
                designed to make me look
                boyish.
        That it seems to suit me.
        That I feel more confident
    with my chest flatter, unlike
    any girl in my class.

    (Or my school or my small town or my life.)

I don't even know if I want to be one.

My parents would think that this means
        I'm gay.
        But I'm not even sure
        if anyone would want me.
        Would want my bound chest.
        Would want this secret.

Every once in a while,
        my friends will say,
                        "That's gay."

        Or my parents will
        wonder,
                        "Why do shows now
                                have so many queers?"
        Like it's a bad thing
        with a word they shouldn't use.

And I think,
        Would they say
        these things
        about me?

But
>> binding feels so good, so right. Like a weight
>> that should hold me down,
>> but lifts me up.

I am confident
>> but cannot be close to anyone,
>> for fear they would say
>> it's wrong.

They could trace the thicker straps,
>> the smooth back, and unusual shape
>> if I'm not careful.
>> So I've given up tight shirts,
>> white shirts, not enough shirts.
>> Added layers.

My secret is buried in more ways than one.
But it is from this depth
that I feel like me.

DOES ANYONE ACTUALLY LIKE GYM CLASS?

Gym class comes, as it does
      in high school. And so
      I change in the big stall.
      Dart out of the cafeteria and confront

the signs.
      You know:
      the man standing tall and
      the woman standing skirted.

I look like neither.
      Long hair pulled back
      into a ponytail, baggy pants
      and a hoodie.

I'm not sure I'm either.
      When I look in the mirror,
      I don't see a girl and
      I don't see a boy. I just see
      my goofy glasses and Beatle-like hair.

This is new,
      the idea of being neither.
      Of being "genderqueer."

And yet, I don't know if this
      is what or who I am.

What does it mean?
        Am I not "Daddy's little girl"?

Do I lose status as daughter?
        Sister? Niece?
        Child? Friend?

If I am neither,
        am I nothing?

This is what I hear
        echoing in my head
        every time I change for gym,
        each time I see those signs.

It's not that I don't
        "fit in."
        There's always a "Hey, Jamie"
        in each class. A friend to sit near.
        To hate homework with or to pair up with
        for a project.

That sometimes makes it harder.
            What would they think?
            Would I be partnerless,
                    powerless,
if I couldn't say whether I was a
                "girl-space-friend" or a
                "boy-space-friend?"

19

NORA

Nora changes
    in the stall next to me.
    (She's got her own
    marks to hide.) And
    it's nice to have class
    together.

She always says she's sorry
    to our friends for not
    being around. And today
    is no different. As we
    stretch before gym, she says,

        "Jamie, I'm sorry I wasn't
            there on Saturday.
        Connor and Colin
        had soccer practice. And
        then I had to make dinner.
        And
        do that paper I had for bio.
        And
        I was so tired." And

she looks brokenhearted,
    like she's saying sorry to herself.

"Nora," I say,
  pretending to stretch.
  More focused on reaching
  for the right words than
  on touching my toes.

"It's okay. We miss you,
  but
  we know it's hard."

This is a lie, and she knows it.
    How could we
    understand the way her
    father works each day,
    drinks each night?

How could we understand
    how her mother chooses
    to miss every day
    with her children?

How could we understand
    how Nora chooses
    to not miss any day
    with her brothers,
    even if we miss her?

Still, we have to say this.
        Have to pretend that
        this is not harder
        than
        our own struggles,
        so that Nora
        feels like she fits.

"God,"
Nora says,
but it's not a prayer.
(She also says
she's given up on the divine
Him/Her/Them/They.)
She finishes:

"I hate gym. It makes me
        so uncomfortable."

Nora is the most thoughtful
        person I know.
        And I know that
        she couldn't know
        (and would be *so sorry* to know)

how I feel watched.
        Looked at. Seen in the
        T-shirt the girls
        have to wear, tighter
        than the boys'.
        Too afraid
                to say, "Hey,
        can you order me the
        boys' shirt
        instead?"

It's much easier to reply
        "me too" and keep
        doing sit-ups,
        to keep going.

SOMETIMES FLANNEL IS A MASK

Mom asked me to help sort
　　　Steve's old clothes.

I think
　　　it's her way of
　　　getting rid
　　　of the ones
　　　she hated.

I imagine
　　　she'll do the same
　　　with mine.

I'm sure
　　　she dreams of me
　　　growing out of this
　　　baggy, boyish
　　　box.

"Can you believe
he used to wear this?"
She holds up an AC/DC shirt
with the sleeves
cut off.
It must be
almost as old as I am.

I laugh, thinking of
        my preppy
        baseball
        brother
        walking around
        with no sleeves.
        "Oh Steve."

Steve made the varsity team
        as a sophomore.
        Started halfway through
        and played second base
        in college.

My brother's a nice guy,
        studies medicine,
        will be the best doctor.
        And I think he's
        the poster child
        for athletes:
        skilled, smart, and
        sensible.

My parents don't want
        me to be Steve.
        And Steve doesn't want
        me to be Steve. But man,
        wouldn't it be easier
        if I was just like him?

Mom pulls out an old flannel shirt.
 And I remember
 teasing Steve
 for looking like
 a lumberjack.

We each took our turn:

Dad:

   "Make sure you chop
   enough wood to make it
   through winter, son!"

Mom:

   "If you're cutting trees down,
   check them for birds first.
   You don't want any nests falling!"

Me:

   "I don't think this is
   what people mean when they say,
   'log in,' Steve."

Now, though,
     I think that flannel might be
     a good look for me.

Women wear flannel. And
     men wear flannel. So
     I could, too.

Mom leaves the room, and
     I pull it out of her pile.
     I start
     a one-shirt stack
     of my own
     where she can't see.

THEY'RE SAD TO SEE ME GO, BUT SOMETIMES I HAVE TO

My parents are used to me
        disappearing on weekends.
        Bouncing between
        coffee shops.

My mother smiles,
        but she looks at me sadly
        as I drive away.
        As if I've already
        left for college.

My father says,

                                "Hey, Jamie,
                                want to go
                                to a movie
                                (or to a bookstore
                                or restaurant
                                or anywhere)?"

Both are so afraid
        to lose their daughter
        when she grows up. But

I'm afraid that
        I'll lose them
        if I tell them my secret.
        If I tell them what
        I leave home
        to think about, alone.

So, on Saturday, I am driving
        further than usual. Out
        to a place
        I've never been
        as a person
        I've never been.

Wearing my brother's flannel,
        which he wore at 14.
        Even though I'm
        almost 17,
        it's still a size
        too big,
        but

it's comfortable.

The shirt feels different. My binder
      keeps me flat. My hair in my hat
      makes me more boy
      than boyish.

I think this
      should make me feel
      better, but I'm not sure
      it's me.

You never know
      until you try,
      right?

I plop
        into a booth,
        coffee in hand.
        Putting my books,
        laptop,
        pens, notepads

        (my whole locker)

        on the table.
        Try to work
        on a paper for English,
        on questions for math,
        on this new identity.

CHANGING MY WORLD

I think that
      I've always felt
      like everyone is
      watching me. As if
      they know
      (because they must know)
      that I'm different.

So today,
      this feeling
      is stronger than ever.
      Like the man at the table
      behind me
      can see through
      my disguise.

Or the woman
      at the counter
      who has seen
      and smiled at me
      knows that I'm a girl
      pretending.

But I'm not.
        I'm not.
        I'm not pretending
        to be anything.
        I'm just trying to
        be myself.

In this shop,
        I turn images of
                myself

                        over

                and

                        over.

What would it be
        to be
        a boy,
                ordering a pastry,
                smiling, talking, working?

I feel like
        this should fit, but
        it doesn't. And
        the reality of
        being a girl
        doesn't either.

What if this is a test
        and the answer is
                all of the above?

What if I am always watched
        but not seen?

What if people always see
        the misfit and don't accept
        the neither?

What if I must always be
        a girl? Or a boy?
        When I'm not one
        or the other.

So I go home,
        having changed
        into my usual clothes
        in the car. And

I sit in my room,
        homework not done.
        And I know
        that I am indeed neither.
        That I was right:
        I'm genderqueer.

SIGN ON THE BINDING LINE

I write it out,
        this new identity,
        this new me,
        this new Jamie.

I watch the
        twist of the "g,"
        the twirl of the "q"
        as ink forms the word
        on the page.

This great new secret,
        the ink rightly binding,
        like a contract.

I even sign my name below.

This leads to a lot and
          a little, all at once.

I am afraid to say anything,
          even though
          nothing would change
          for those around me.

It's about me,
          but I know
          it can't be
          (it isn't)
          that simple.

And so it starts,
       this process
       of being new.

Every day, I find
       something new
       that tells me
       I must either be a
       boy or a girl:

the bathroom signs,
       clothing stores,
       "Ladies and Gentleman,"
       birthday cards,
       Christmas cards.
       Even toothbrushes
       have a binary gender—
       that is, male or female.

What about me?
　　I am left out,
　　and no one sees
　　the problem.

Thankfully, no one questions
　　when I use the women's room
　　or when I buy boy's this
　　and girl's that,
　　a hodgepodge mix.

THERE ARE MOMENTS WHEN I WANT TO SHOUT

I don't want
    to keep
    this secret.
    It's tiring,
    and I don't
    want to be alone.

I don't want
    to tell all
    of my friends though,
    either. So what do
    I do?

Nora would be
        wonderful. Of course
        she would.

Eric's so busy with
        swimming. And
        I'm not sure
        how he'd react.

Levi, though.
        My genderqueerness
        is not the same
        as his gayness. But

he was told men only love
        women and defies it.
        And I was told
        there are only
        men and women
        and defy it.

WE'RE A SMALL GANG

When I met Levi,
        he told me that
        Levi jeans were
        only for him.

I said,
        "That's not true."
        And he paused,
        thinking.
        (As six-year-olds do.)

                "Okay. You can wear them
                        if you want."

That was first grade. And
        we've moved together
        to middle and then
        high school, collecting
        friends for our
        little gang.

We're an odd mix
        of people.
        And my parents joke
        that, secretly, we rule
        the school.

Levi and I laugh about this.
        Where did
        they go
        to school if
        they think
        we're popular?

It all happened by accident:

Jason lived next door to Levi.
        And he sat with Nora
        on her first day
        as the new kid. And
        I came along with Levi.

Callie and Eric came next
        in junior high. And then
        she and Jason started dating
        last year.

Levi's been there,
      always. After he came out,
      he told me that
      he had a crush on
      my brother Steve.

And, although
      Steve is straighter
      than the pitches
      he throws,
      there's a part of me
      that still hopes that
      Levi could be
      my brother-in-law
      one day.

A COMING OUT

I text Levi a week after
      my identity becomes
      clear to me.

(I wanted to give it time
      to sink in.)

(I wanted to give myself time
      to sink in.)

"Hey."
(I text.)

"Hey, J, what's up?"
(Levi answers.)

"Can we hang out soon?"

"Yeah! I miss you."

"Okay.
I have something to tell you."

"Is everything okay?"

"Yeah, I think so."

"Wednesday?"

"After school?"

"Yes"

"Perfect."

"<3"

"<3"

I know Levi
        is the least likely
        to judge me. But
        I'm still pacing
        when he picks me up.

We go to our place,
        since it's still
        warm enough
        to hike
                down
                        to the
                                water.

"It feels like it's
            been forever since
            we were last here."
I say, looking for
            skipping stones.
            My usual habit.

                    "Yeah, this year's been
                            crazy. I can't
                            remember
                            the last time
                            Eric was with us,"
                    Levi says.

"I wish he'd quit the swim team."

                    "Me too."

I should
start. Even Levi
seems nervous.
Instead, I ask,

"How's Evan?"

Levi smiles,
"He's really
good."

"Good."

Then silence.

"So Levi, I,
      I don't…"

Breathe, I tell myself.

"I don't think,
I know that
I'm not,
I'm not a girl."

Halfway there.

"I'm also not a boy."

So…

"I'm genderqueer."

Levi doesn't
      let me catch
      my breath
      before smiling and saying,
      "Okay, cool."

He hugs me,
      starts crying with me.
      (This is normal.)
      Says, "Congrats."
      Makes this day a celebration.

After all, he knows how to
      come out.

He does not:
> say "I knew it,"
> ask what that means,
> hate me.

He does:
> say "I'm proud of you,"
> ask how I knew,
> love me.

IT'S NICE TO FEEL NORMAL

Like this is
normal and
  okay.

Levi is set
  on making sure
  I know all of this
  to be true.

By the end of the day,
  we shout over the small,
  man-made waterfall:
  "We're here, and
  we're queer."

I tell him
        how scared I am,
        how I like this identity,
        how I don't know
        how to explain it to
                anyone else. But

with each nod,
        I hear him say,
                        "I know,
                                it's going to be okay."

"So what about
          pronouns?"
Levi asks this
as he weaves the car
out of the park.
          "How should I refer to you?"

I had thought
          about this.
          It's a question
          that pops up
          (according to Google).

"'She' is feminine,
    but I guess
    I'm okay
    with it."
I pause. "But
I think I prefer 'they.'"

"They"
    doesn't have
    a gender, so
    even though
    it means more than one,
    I like it.

        "Whatever you want, J.
        I just want you
            to be happy."

I get out
      of the car, back
      at school, where
      I left mine to drive together.

Levi stops, promises me that
      even though
      this will be hard
           ("And it will be,
                  which sucks, so I'm sorry."),
      he's there.

I hug him again,
      squeeze his hand,
      and I get out of the car.

And that's the
      first time
           I come out.

Levi doesn't tell
        Evan or
        anyone. Even though
        it'd almost
        be easier if I let him.

I get home
        from our hike, and
        my mom asks
        how it was.

"Really great.
        It's been so long
        since I've seen Levi."

She winks, I think,
        as I go into my room.
        Which
        makes me laugh.
        If only she knew.

IN THE CLOSET BUT ON THE ROAD

I start telling Levi
      everything.
      We drive
           further and further
               out on day trips.

Sometimes
      he brings Evan,
      who I loop in because
      Levi is
      my best friend, and
      Evan is important
      to him and so
      to me.

We go to Rochester
        when we can.
        Hide in this city
        just up the I-90.
        Exist in a place where
        our secrets
        don't matter.

Evan and Levi
        walk up East Avenue,
        get ice cream,
        kiss in front of
        pride flags.

"J!" Levi laughs,
        and I don't think
        I've ever
        seen him so happy.
"This restaurant has
        gender-neutral restrooms!"

He points at a little café.
        We come back once,
        twice, as often as we can.

Walking in, it feels
     the same as the shops
     back home. But

I wander back, past
     bulletin boards of LGBT+
     events and
     things I want to do.

Toward two doors that are
     the same. No little man.
     No little woman.

I get to choose.

THE THINGS I NEVER THOUGHT TO THINK ABOUT

I ask Levi
  a million questions
  about being gay or
  about gender or
  anything, really.

"Why doesn't
  genderqueer have
  a letter in 'LGBT+?'"

"Should I change my name?
  Jamie is both a boy's name
  and a girl's name though…"

"Does this mean I'm gay? A lesbian?"

Levi doesn't give me
answers. He says,

    "Jamie."
        He places one hand
        on my shoulder.
        Weaves
        our fingers together.
    "You have to decide
        some of this for
        yourself."

    "Whatever you decide—
        Jamie, James,
        gay, straight,
        whatever—
        it's okay."

Sitting up
        past midnight,
        my dog at the end
        of my bed,

I do a lot
        of research.
        Find that
        genderqueer is new.

Decide to
        keep my name.
        And decide to not think
        too much
        about romance,
        not yet.

(One coming out
        at a time.)

Everyone else is asleep,
        but my world is
        changing.

I tell this to Levi,
        and he nods.
                "Sounds good."

It's simple
        and it's easy
        to think that
        I need his approval.

But
        I'm trying
        to make sure
        that I think about
        my happiness, too.

(I'm much happier
        just being able
                to talk about it.)

HITTING THE BOOKS

I've spent days
      on the floor
      of my room.
      Only getting up
      to refill my water bottle or
      pull a new book
      off of my shelf.

Now,
      I look for the
      "books of my people,"
      stories about gender,
      sexuality.

I lose myself there,
     spend hours
     with new heroes.

Even *A Midsummer Night's Dream*
     makes my list:
     Puck seems
     a little queer to me.

I pretend
     there are more
     like me
     who
     blend girl and boy,
     pink and blue, to
     make purple.

Each morning,
     I bind.
     And while Levi
          grows closer
               to me,

I still keep
     this secret
     for me alone.

It's never come up,
     even in the endless
     hours of
     driving.

I suppose
          that I still
          feel shame. Like
          I'm denying

something natural
          by tucking and
          tightening
          my chest. But

it's too
          comforting, like
          the tightness
          is a sign that
          I finally fit.

IT WOULD BE NICE

to not be
      the only "they"
      that I know,

and it seems like
      college will be
      my escape.

But that's a year away,
      and I still haven't
      said anything
      to my parents.

Talking to Levi helped.
      And sometimes I think
      that coming out can
      fix the secret. But I will
      still be alone,
      will still be the only
      "they."

It would be nice
        to find someone
        who understands

what it is

        to wear a "they/them" pin
                each day. Or

        to correct those that ignore
                this pin. Or

        to choose a restroom. Or

        to say "hey, y'all" instead of
                "hey, guys." Or

        to be tired by
                gendered things. Or

        to do so many things.

MY FAVORITE BOOKSTORE, RENEWED

I look for
      others
      online.
      People who bind.
      People who understand.
      So

when I hear of a poet
      who's like me
      (genderqueer!)
      coming to
      Buffalo,

I tell my parents
      I have to go
      for a project. And
      drive into the city.

I don't ask Levi
     or Evan or
     Nora or
     anyone
     to come—

this is for me.

My dad brought me here
        when I was younger.
        A small bookshop tucked
        into a small
        neighborhood.

He knew I'd love it.
        This little corner of the block.
        This little corner of the world.

It was small. The
        spines on shelves
        were a puzzle of other places.

I always believed
        in other universes.
        Of places and lives
        we couldn't imagine. Except
        here they were in this store,

and I could go
        to each one.

My father is
        a scientist,
        does research
        on cancer,
        comes home tired,
        often stressed.

But here, in this store,
        he told me
        stories that
        I think
        he wanted
        science to prove.

Tonight, I will
      see a life
      like the one
      I am scared to have.

I slip into the back,
      leaning right.
      I pass the shoulders
      of those taller than me.

People holding books
      of poetry like
      the one I just bought.

They are waiting calmly
      while, for some reason,
      I am nervous.

Yet at the same time I'm home
        because some of these
        people look like
        people, not just
        men and women.

That is, they look like me.
        Or, rather,
        I look like them.

Finally.

The poet is not
        loud.
        Does not write only
        on their gender.
        Is simply
        living their life.

Their hair is
        cut short,
        whisps coming out
        of the sides of their red hat.
        It matches their lipstick,

which matches
        the red of a bow tie
        around their neck.

They still look formal,
        in a dress shirt
        and suspenders, which sit
        on shoulders that

I think may hold
        some of my hopes.

They speak
        softly, lips barely
        touching
        the microphone.
        Smiling
                as they read.

We all hear them though,
        as they speak
        on gender,
        on genderqueerness,
        on being looked at twice.

Yes, I am so afraid of that, too.

Maybe, one day,
        I could speak like this.
        Could talk about binding
        like it's normal,
        like it's okay.
        Because it is.
        (I just have to accept that.)

They sign books
        at the end,
        kindly greet each
        of us, ask our names
        and

our pronouns. So
        I shyly say,

"Hi, Jamie.
        That is, *I'm* Jamie, and
I use they/them."

They shake my hand,
     like they know
     what I'm going through.
     And then I remember,
     they do.

               "It's nice to meet you, Jamie.
                    Thanks for coming."

And they wink
     as they hand
     my book back.

YOU LEARN SOMETHING NEW EVERY DAY

"That's the gay wink,"
        Levi concludes
        when I tell him.

I look at him funny
        and he continues,
        "No, I know you aren't gay.
        I'm just referring
        to the whole
        LGBT+ community.

And some people choose
        to say 'gay'
        to sum it up.

Anyway, LGBT+ humans
        tend to know
        when they're in
        good company,
        so they'll wink or nod.

It happens to
        Evan and I sometimes."

"Sure," I reply,
        like it doesn't matter,
        but it's the first time
        a stranger knows.
        And it's the first time
        a stranger still smiles at me.

The book slides
        onto my shelf
        in the way
        I wish to fit in—
        easily.

I'M NOT EVEN OUT OF BED YET

"Knock, knock, Jamie,"
        says my dad,
        pushing the door
        and coming in.

It's Saturday,
        and I'm barely awake.
        Still lying in bed,
        reading poetry.

He sits down
        on the edge
        of the mattress,
        like he always does.

"I always forget
        how bad
        your breath is
        in the morning."
He laughs. Dad humor.
        "What are you reading?"

"Just a poet
        I like."

It's the one
          from the reading.
          I haven't been
          able to leave it
          alone for more than a day.
He gestures for it,
          wants to see it.
          An innocent request.

So I hand it over.

                    "This is…different."
                    He's looking
                    at the poet's picture,
          "This…" He pauses. "…person
                    has an interesting look."

               Then he shrugs,
                    "Have fun with it.
                    You always find
                    interesting things
                    to read."
I can't read him
          though.

What does "different" mean?
          "Interesting"?
          Why did he pause before "person"?

NOT READY

"Jamie."
My mom welcomes me home
from school.
"How was your day?"

"School was fine," I reply,
    walking past her
    to my room. And
    it's true.

School's fine.
    I keep my friends
    close
    and I go to my
    nerdy club meetings,
        choir and the newspaper,
        hang out with Levi and Evan.

No one really knows,
        but someone does,
        and I know
        where to find
        others like me
        (my bookshelf).
                And, for now,
                that's good,

even if I'm dreaming
        of not hiding.

                        "I haven't seen many
                                of your friends
                                lately.
                                Just Levi.
                                        Is everything okay?"

"Oh yeah," I reply,
        but feel
        guilty right away.
        "Everything's good.
        They've just been busy."

I text Levi that night:

"Do you think that
I should tell
everyone?
Well,
our friends."

 "Sort of?"

"What do you mean?"

 "Maybe…
 I mean,
 have YOU thought
 about telling
 everyone?"

"Umm, not really?"

 "Why not?"

"I'm not ready."

 "That's okay,
 but it might be
 good,
 you know?"

"I'll think
about it."

It's a Friday,
and I don't talk
to Levi for a few days.

Why
        would he think
        that I'm ready?

Why
        would he push
        me like this?

I'm not ready,
        I'm not ready,
                I'm not ready.

Right?

I liked the sureness
        of my life.
        Was okay,
        I thought.
        But I'm still living
        a secret.

What if
        my parents
        don't want me?
        Leave me like
        Nora's mom left her?

What if
        I was alone?

Where would I go?

Who would I be
        if I was nothing
        to them?

And Levi doesn't even know
        about the binding.

I don't even know
        if it's temporary
        or if this is what I'll do
        forever.

I'd have to buy
        a real binder.
        Because what I'm doing
        isn't good for me,
        can have real effects
        on my health,
        like hurting my spine
        or messing up my breathing.

        But

how can I do that
        without someone knowing?
        And

how can I do that
        without them thinking
        I'm a freak?

It's night,
     of course,
       when I wonder if
       Levi's awake still.

Maybe he even knows
       that I'm upset with him.

But I don't want to
       tell him this.
       Don't want to feel
       this pressure.

Don't want to be
       embarrassed of
       the pressure on my chest.

And

I'm not ready.

THE TALK

I'm eating breakfast when
      Mom asks:

                     "Are you dating
                     Levi?
                     Is that why you spend
                     so much time
                     together?"

I nearly spit
      out my toast,
      "No, Mom,
      that's definitely not it."

                     "Do you want to?"

"Date Levi?"

                     "Yes. That's perfectly normal."

Oh, Mother.

"No, he's just
my best friend."

"Okay."

"Okay."

"I'm here if…"

"Mom."

"Have a nice day, Jamic."

My parents never had
        "the talk"
        with me.

And they don't know
        Levi's gay.

But they are good friends
        with his parents,
        so I can't trust them
        not to share his secret.

We never talk about romance.
        And as I drive to school,
        listening to another
        radio commercial
        about car insurance,

I realize that
        it was probably hard
        for her to ask.
        I was a normal teen
        (for once),

and maybe she's trying.
        And maybe she'd be okay
        one day.

Maybe.

Levi corners me
        as I wait in line
        for a muffin before
        first period.

He's never been afraid
        to have hard talks
        with me, so
        I knew
        this was coming.

Even though I didn't
        expect to *talk talk*
        at 7:30 a.m.

NOT THE SORT TO STAY MAD AT

Levi says,
    "You're mad at me."

I shrug.

"I guess I didn't like
how you responded."

                "I didn't mean
                to pressure you."

"Well…"

                "I'm sorry, J.
                    You should
                    take your time."

I soften.
"It's okay, Lev.
I'm just not ready,
okay?"

                "Absolutely."
                    He pays
                    for my muffin
                    and

                    before everyone else
                    arrives, he adds,

"I'm thinking of
telling my parents."

"Oh?"

"Yeah, Evan's thinking
the same thing."
He looks down,
          peels the orange
          he'd bought for himself.

"We've been talking
about it for a while."

"You know
I support you."

"I'm thinking of
telling them tonight."

I breathe,
feel the air move
down and in,
past my binder.
(I can always feel it.)
And then
up and out.
"Wow."

                "Yeah."
                    He finishes peeling,
                    pops a wedge
                    into his mouth. Says,
                "Jason said I could
                    stay with him, if…"

"Do you think…?"

                He shrugs,
                    his shoulders shifting
                    the weight of the world.
                "I don't know,
                    honestly."

"What will you do,
just go to Jason's?"

          "I wrote myself
          a letter. Promising
          that I wouldn't
          hide if
          Mom and Dad wanted me to."

I smile,
          reach for
          his shoulder.
"And Evan?"

          "Eric offered him
          the same deal.
          Both of them being
          on the swim team helped."

He laughs.
    "I don't think this
    is what my dad meant
    when he said
    to be a
    'guys' guy.'"

"It's all his fault."

    "Oh yes, definitely."

It's crazy,
    this feeling of
    sending Levi off
    to do something
    I can't. And

I hope that
    I'll joke like he does
    when I do.

FRIENDS JUST WANT TO HAVE FUN

A stress ball lands
      between us.
           Jason catches it
           when Levi returns
           the volley.

Our friends have arrived,
      just as I get settled
      at our table. I
peel an orange, then hear:

                  "What's up, y'all?"
                  Eric grabs a wedge of orange. Says,
                  "Jamie, I feel like
                      it's been ages."

"Sorry, it's been
so long."

"Nah, it's okay."
                Eric's the most
                laid-back of us.
                Even though
                his parents put
                the most pressure
                on him.
                        "We've all got
                        stuff going on."

"Like that paper for
        Mr. Evenhouse?"
                Jason throws
                the stress ball up.
                Then fixes
                his backpack strap
                before catching the ball.

"That was brutal,
        I don't think
        I'll ever forget
        how to spell
        'guillotine'
        after that."

"Eight pages on
the French Revolution
was seven pages too many,"
Nora agrees.
"I never thought
I'd miss government."

"Anyway," says Callie,
(who's taking AP Euro History,
far scarier than our class),
"Can we all go
see a movie this weekend?"

I quickly agree,
"That'd be great."

"You and Levi
        aren't running off
        to something?"
                Jason asks,
                kind of harshly.

"Jamie is my beard
when I'm out
with Evan,"
        Levi says, ignoring
        Jason's tone.

I'm not sure
who's covering
for whom.

"A movie sounds great,"
Nora says.
"I already set a playdate
for the twins
with some neighborhood
kids."

Nora looks thrilled,
a night off
from mothering her brothers.

Eric says,
"Just give me time
to nap after practice
in the morning, and
I'm all set to go."
Poor Eric, having to sport.

I don't tell him
that I'd cry if
I had to rise with the sun
to go swimming. Thinking,
*Binders can't even go
in the water.*

"Okay, Saturday at six, then?"
Callie settles this.
"Speaking of time,
I'm off to class."

We split into pairs,
Eric and Callie to English,
Jason and Nora to Spanish,
and Levi and I to chemistry.

"My mom asked if
we were dating,"
I say.

"What'd you say?"
Levi asks.

"That that's not the case."

"Does she think…?"
He looks at me,
and nearly bumps
into the guy in front of him,
forgetting high school
hallway traffic
for a moment.

"She's got no clue."
I roll my eyes,
"I don't even think
she believed me,
to be honest."

"That's good," he says.

"Can't spill the beans early."

"It'll be okay, Lev."

"Let's not talk
        about it anymore,
        okay?"

"Sure,
but
let me know
if you change your mind?
And what happens?"

"Of course."
        He reaches down,
        squeezes my hand
        in the crowded hall.
                "Thanks, J."

CAN YOU HEAR ME BREATHING?

"My Dad's bowling later.
Want to come over?"
Nora asks
while we run
the mile in gym.
"It's been so long
since we hung out.
We could watch a movie
and do homework?"

"Sure,"
　　I agree,
　　not wanting to add
　　to the idea that
　　I prefer Levi to
　　everyone else.

　　(Right now,
　　though,
　　I do).

"Great!
The twins will be happy
to see you!"
Her face lights up,
and I feel guilty that
I haven't told her.
(And that I'm still not going to.)

"Just let me know
when he's gone, and
I'll come over."

"That's perfect.
Thanks
for understanding."

We stop talking
after that because we've got a 10-minute limit
or else we have to run it again.
Something about state standards,
I guess.

The binder makes this
harder. And
I become aware
of how loudly
I'm breathing.

Can everyone hear me?
The up and down
of my chest.
The in and out
of air.

Sometimes,
people comment on
how loudly I breathe.
And that means they know
that there's something
different
          about me.

Never, though,
would they be able to guess.

Nora keeps pace
        with me, even though
        I think she's faster.
        And
        it would be nice
        to tell her. To ask her
        if I breathe loudly.
        To have her
        help me
        cover it
        with chitchat.

But Nora,
        Nora has enough—
        her father,
        her brothers.
She doesn't need to
        worry about me,
        too.

OTHER PEOPLE HAVE PROBLEMS, TOO

Later that night,
    I park
    on the street,
    then shoulder
        my backpack.

      Nora's already texted
        to say,

                "Dad's gone."

So I don't knock,
just walk in
like I have
since I was a kid.
Before Connor and Colin
      were born.
Before Nora's
    dad's drinking.

"Jamie!"
                    "Jamie!"
Connor and Colin barrel
        through when they hear
        the door open.
                Little

                        cartoons

                                running.

(I can't even see which feet
                        belong to which boy.)

"Hey, boyos!"
        I say.
        They laugh at
        their nickname.
"What are we watching?"

        I don't catch
        the name of
        the cartoon movie

        but I follow

                them into the

                        living room.

117

"Do you mind
                watching this?"
                        Nora asks shyly.
        "It's the easiest
                way to keep them
                        occupied."

"Of course not!"
        I quickly reply,
                h e f t i n g
                        my backpack
                                down
        onto the nearest sofa.

I follow it,
        crossing my legs
        on her carpet.
        Using cushions as a desk.

"Definitely don't want to
do this trig homework."

                "Oh, you and me both, J."

Nora and I used to
    spend hours
        in her home.

    Her dad taught me
        how to do
            my multiples of nine
            on my hands:

            "If you want to do
                two times nine—

"That's eighteen, Mr. Richards."

            He laughed,
            "Well, yes, but
            if you put your
            second finger down,
                the tens come before
                    the space,
                and the ones after it."

"So...I have one before
    and
        eight after."

            "Which is eighteen!"

"Eighteen!"

119

Mr. Richards started
        drinking a few years
            ago

(right after the twins
were born),

                    and Nora's never said
                    why.

        It's nice to be here,

                    to listen
                    to Connor and Colin.

        Because Nora will say
            anything

                        so she can feel like
                        her life is

                            normal.

And, tonight, it's nice to be
the one supporting,
        rather than
        the one needing
        support.

I keep my phone
next to me in case
Levi needs anything.

"What's been happening
in your life?"
Nora asks, sitting
in the corner
of the couch,
knees up as a desk
while she works.

"Not much,"
I lie.
"Steve's coming home
to visit this weekend."

"That'll be fun!"

"Yeah!
It'll be nice to see him."

"I haven't seen him
in ages."

"Since before he left
for college?"

"Yeah, he was always
so fun when we were
kiddos."

"I'll tell him you say
hi.'"

SECRETS TAKE UP SO MUCH SPACE

The thing about Nora
      is that
      she's such a
      gossip.

She's so
      sweet
      and
      caring

that people tell
      her
      everything.
      So she
      (always)
      knows what's
      going on.

We update each other
      on what
      we've heard:
      Johnny's doing *that*,
      Miguel's going to college *there*,
      and Sofie's dating *her*.

It's not that
          we really care
          or will share
          secrets outside
          of our friends.

We just like to know.
          But it tastes
          funny tonight.

This is the first
          time I've had
          my own
          gossip-worthy
          secret. So I say,

"Can we not talk
          about this stuff?"

                              "Oh." Nora's surprised.
                              "Sure,
                                        is everything okay?"

"Yeah, I just
          don't feel like it."

Not too much later,
     Nora's dad calls
     and says to
     warm up
     dinner. So

I leave.

When I get home,
     I text Nora
     from the car
     and thank her.
     Promise that
     everything is good
     between us and that
     I hope her dad
     wasn't too hard on her.

I still haven't heard
     from Levi,
     so I send a
     "<3"

My *Ghostbusters* ringtone sounds.

It's past midnight,
        but I always sleep
        with my phone on loud.

"Hello?"

                        "J!"

"Lev?"
        I sit up.
        "Oh my God,
        Lev!"

                        "It went well!"
                                He answers before
                                I can even ask.

"They were okay?"

                        "Yes! I'm still crying,
                                I'm so happy."

"What happened?"

                        "Jamie, it was so good.
                                They said
                                they loved me
                                and they want me
                                no matter what.
                                That this
                                doesn't change *anything*."

"And Evan?"

                  Levi pauses.
                        There's a shift here,
                        like he feels he can't
                        be happy anymore.
                        "He's at Eric's.
                                His parents
                                don't want him
                              around his sister."

I don't say
        that this
        scares me,

that I stop
        breathing
        for a second.

Because what if
        what if
        what if
        this is what happens to me?

I say,
        "Levi…
        I'm so sorry."

Like I'm also
        apologizing
        to myself.

Then, there's not much to say, so I add:

"Maybe you should
        get some sleep?"

"Yeah, you're right."
              I listen to him yawn.

I try to do
the same thing.

Evan is
        sweet,
        kind,
        scared,
        lost, and
        at Eric's.

I dream of
        being him.
        I wake up
        sweating,
        afraid that

I saw the future.

AT THE MOVIES

It takes us too long
        to figure out
        whose turn it is
        to pick the movie.

And we're all quiet
        as we try to explain
        why we haven't
        seen each other
        so much.

Like it's a secret
        we're keeping
        from one another.

(Of course, for me,
        it is.)

"Levi just came out to
        his parents.
    He should choose the movie."
                    Jason asserts this like
                    Fred in *Scooby-Doo*
                    saying,
                    "Well, gang,
                    let's split up and
                    search for clues."

    "Yeah, you're right,"
            says Callie. And
            we all agree.

Will they celebrate me
        like this?

Or will I be like Evan,
        whose situation
        we don't talk about,

too sad to celebrate?

We each buy tickets.
>> Then Jason and I collect
>>> money for snacks.
>> Eric and Callie go
>>> to get seats.
>>> (Callie will pick the best ones.
>>> And Eric is confident enough
>>> to save them.) And
>> Nora and Levi always
>>> go to the bathroom
>>> before a movie.

It's always fun
>> to see our routine
>> in action.
>> Our little family.

When the lights come up,
    I stand and stretch
       between Nora and Levi.
    We compare notes
        on the movie.

                "Guys, my feet are asleep!"
                    Eric whines.
            (This, too, is routine.)
            And Callie kicks him.
            (So is that.)

We file out to the parking lot
    and part for the weekend.
    Eric, Jason, and Callie
        each have practice tomorrow.
    Nora's got the twins.
    Levi's out with Evan.
    I'm hiding out
        to write a paper.

                We promise not to go
                    so long that we forget
                    again.

Levi and I carpooled.
  He looks at me.
    "I see you, J.
      What're you thinking about?"

"I miss them."

     "Me too.
      Do you think Evan
       fits in?"

"Yeah,"
  I agree quietly,
  hoping that
  my coming out
  is as well-received.
"We all love him..."

    "I'm going to bring him
    more when we're
    with everyone. I think…"
      Levi pauses, and I see his
      guilt for being accepted by
      his family when Evan isn't.

    "I think he could use it.
      Some more people
      on his side,
      I mean."

"He's got us.
It's going to be okay."

I go home and
try to be as confident as I sound.

STEVE COMES HOME

A few years ago,
      Steve used to
      drive home from college
      in just enough time
      to pick me up
      from school.

He'd yell
      for me
      as I tried
      to get on
      the bus

because he knew
      I'd forget
      which day
      he was coming home.

Now,
      he still tries
      to surprise me,
      even though I drive myself.

Except
      he's usually
      not very good
      at it.

Today,
        he catches me
                on the stairs. He springs
                from the closet
                underneath them.

I nearly fall
        down. Then, laughing, I
        hug him. And he comes

upstairs with me
        to chat.

And then,
        we're sitting
        on the bed when
        he notices:

                "Is that my old
                        Beatles shirt?"

He tugs on my sleeve,
        shows taped straps,
                asks,

                "Jamie, why is there
                tape on something
                under this?"

Oh crap.

My first thought is to say
     it's "a girl thing."
     But not only
     is it a lie,
     it's so...*gender*-filled.

So I

     fix my shirt.
     Pull it back into place.
     Try to
          stop
          the panicked
          beatbeatbeatbeatbeat
          of my heart.

          Breathe.
          Please, just breathe.

                    "Jamie, it's okay.
                       Whatever it is,
                       it's okay."

And I remember
     how well
     Steve knows me.

"You're panicking.
        Don't—it's okay."

"Have you heard
        of people
        who bind their chest?"

        I prepare to explain.

                "Yes."

I pause. "What?"

                "I have a friend
                        who is transgender.
                He binds his chest
                        to look more
                        like a guy."

"Oh."

                "Is that what—"
                        Steve motions to me,
                                "that's for?"

"Yeah…"
        I shrug.

"There are better ways,
        I know.
        But how could I tell
        Mom and Dad?"

                            "This isn't good for you,
                                    Jame."
                            The mention of
                            my nickname
                            makes me feel
                            worse.
                            "I mean, binding's
                                    totally okay."

"What?"
        I look up
                from the floor
                for the first time
                in what feels like
                        h o u r s.
"You're not
        disappointed?"

                            "Oh no, kiddo."
                                    Steve leans against
                                            my bed.
                            "You do you.
                                    I'm kind of
                                            curious about
                                            why you do it.
                            But it's okay
                                    as long as
                                    you're doing it
                            safely."

I look at Steve,
      drop my jaw,
      catch some flies,
      blink.
(Every cliché
      about being
      surprised
      becomes real.)

So, of course,
      thinking he
      might be
      okay,
      I risk it:

"I'm genderqueer."

                "Cool."

"Yeah?"

                "Of course,
                    Jamie.
                Do you want
                    to talk more about it?"

So I tell him
      everything.
      And suddenly, Levi's not
          the only one to
             know.

WHY I KEEP MY OLDER BROTHER AROUND

My mom knocks
    20 minutes
    later.
She's happy, I think,
that Steve and I
    are so close.

        "Steve, honey,
           where do you
                want to go
         for dinner?"

        "Ah,"

           he says.
           Pauses.
           Thinks.

        Then,
        (finally)
        so as to keep her out,
           replies,
        "Something with tacos?"

           She accepts this. Says,
        "Oh, there's this
           great place that just
           opened…"

She keeps talking,
        then her voice fades
                down the stairs.

                        "I'm assuming
                        Mom and Dad
                        don't know?"
                                Steve asks.

"No, and
        I don't want them to
        right now.

I don't even know
        how to
        explain
        it."

                "Okay,
                        take your time.
                                I do think
                                        that they'll be
                                        alright with it,
                                                if
                                                that
                                                helps."

"It does.
Thanks,
Steve."

I'm tired,
        and I think
        that we're done.
        Then Steve says:

                        "I'm gonna be here
                                for about a
                                        week.
                        Why don't I
                                order
                                a real binder
                                for you?

                        They won't see
                                the charge.

                        Won't open
                                packages
                                for me…"

"…won't know."

                        "Exactly.
                                They won't know.

"Steve…
        would you mind?

That would make
        my life
        so much
        better."

                        "Of course.
                                Just email me
                                        a link tonight."

141

"I'll make sure it gets here
before I leave."

I get up
        and hug Steve.
        I cry
                (finally).

                "I have your back,
                kiddo."
                He rests
                        his head
                                on mine.
                "Just always
                        remember:
                        you're everything
                                you need to be
                                right now
                                and
                                it's enough."

I am everything I need to be right now and it's enough.

Steve goes downstairs.
    Plays his role as
    the visiting child.

And I sink
    into
            my bed
    and breathe.

Going from fear
    to validation
                to fear
                    to acceptance

    in such a short
    time

drained me.
            But
            Steve was okay.

At least one
    person
    in my family
        is okay with it

                        (with me).

I grab my phone
        to tell Levi.
        Happy to keep up
        the streak
                of happy coming-outs.

"Steve knows!"
(I text.)

                                    "An '!' means
                                    it's OK,
                                    right?"
                                    (Levi answers.)

"Yes!

He was so nice
        about it!

He said
        he has a trans friend
        that uses
        different pronouns
        that I could
        talk to
        about gender stuff!"

                            "J, that's awesome!"

"I feel so good
        about it!"

                        "Yes!
                            It's such a
                                good feeling."
144

SOMETIMES MY MOM MAKES ME WANT TO JUMP OUT OF A MOVING VEHICLE

My mom likes
> to surprise me
> in the car.

Our large SUV
> in which
> I learned to drive.

(Though I have
> my own,
> much smaller,
> car named Chip).

I think it's because
> she knows
> I can't escape.

When my grandparents
		got a divorce,
		she told me
		on the
		ride home
				from the bookstore.

When she was laid off (for two, too-long months)
		just before
				I started
				high school,
		she told me
		after treating me
				to ice cream.

Tonight,
		we're riding
		home
				from the mall.
		(I needed
		new jeans.)

"So I ran into
Evan Holmes'
mother at the store
yesterday."

It's impressive
how her eyes
never leave the road
but she still seems
able to *look*
at me.

I brace myself.

"Oh?"

"She said he's dating Levi!"

"Yeah…"

"I didn't know he was
gay."

"Does it matter?"

147

I don't want this
        to be
        an important talk.
But I can feel myself
        putting weight
        on her reaction,
as if it will
        predict my future.

            "I mean, no.
                It's different.
            But I thought you and he…"

"Why's it different?"
        I look at
        the lines on my hand
        like a palm reader.

        What will my future be?

"We just don't have
a lot of
people who are gay
in our town."
She huffs.
"Jamie, I didn't bring this up
to be criticized."

"Why'd you
bring it up?"

What was it that Steve told me to remember?

"Because I thought
you and Levi
were dating."

"We aren't."
I shrug.
And she does it again—
eyes on the road
but looking at me.

Oh, yeah. I am everything I need to be right now and it's enough.

"Why'd you let me
think you were?"

"I didn't mean to."
I didn't stop it,
since she kept
bringing it up.

I am everything I need to be right now and it's enough.

"Okay. Just…
    sometimes I feel like
    you're lying to me,
    Jamie. And I don't
    want that."

"I'm not lying
    to you, Mom."

She nods,
    "I was sorry
    to hear
    Evan was kicked out.
    And I told Mrs. Holmes so."

MY MOM HAS MORE PROS THAN CONS

I grab
>   the bag of new jeans,
>   thank my mother,
>   and hurry inside
>>   to overthink
>>   and panic.

Why did it seem
>   like she was hiding
>>   her thoughts?

Why does it matter
>   that we don't have
>   a lot of people
>   who are gay
>   in our town?

Why does she seem
>   disappointed
>   that Levi isn't
>   my boyfriend?

At least,
        I think,
she said she was sorry to hear about Evan.

And from there,
        flows a list of positives:

She didn't say
        it was bad
        to be gay.

She didn't say
        anything mean
        about
        my best friend.

She didn't say,

                        "Jamie, you better not
                                be different."

She didn't see
        the secret
        in my head. And

she wants
        the truth,
        so she can't be mad
        when (if) I tell her.

These are all good things.

I repeat again:

        I am everything I need to be right now and it's enough.

WHEN THE TRUTH BANGS AT THE DOOR

The subject of Levi and Evan
            comes up
            at dinner
            the next night.

Steve's still here,
            and we're sitting
            in our dining room.

That's unusual
            in general,
            but when Steve's here,
            we do a lot of family things.

                        "Oh, that's great,"
                                    Steve says,
                                    when mom announces
                                    Levi's relationship.
                                    "Good for them.
                                    It takes a lot of
                                                courage to
                                                come out."

I smile and say,
            "They're really happy
            that they did."
            Like I'm just talking about
                        the boys.

                        "Yes, it does,"
                                    my father says.

153

"My college roommate
        didn't come out
        until much later,"
Steve says.

"When Charlie came out
        as trans,
        it was really rough
        with his family."
My brother is untouchable,
        and he knows it,
        so he adds,
"Which I think is unfair."

"Trans?"
Mom asks.

"Transgender,"
        I manage to say,
        much more carefully.

        Steve says,
                "Charlie was born
                as a female biologically,
                but he identifies as male."

        "Interesting…"
                Mom says.

        She doesn't seem too
        pleased.
                Spears a tomato
                in her salad,
                        changes
                        the subject.

Steve stops by
     my room later
     after everyone else
     goes to bed.

          "Hey, kiddo."

"Hey, kidbro."

          "How are you
               doing?
            Dinner was…
              interesting."

It doesn't help
     that he says
          "interesting"
     like she did,
     even though
     he probably
          doesn't realize.

"What if Mom
     hates me?"

          "Mom's not going
             to hate you."

"Steve…
     you saw her
     tonight."

          "She adores you.
          She brags about you,
          tells me that you're great."

"Steve."
    I repeat,
            frustrated.
    I'm allowed to feel this,
            to fear that.

                "I know it's scary."

                        He breathes,
                        "Okay, it's not
                                something
                                I've had to
                                think
                                about.
                        But the thought
                                of coming out
                                scares me,
                        so I can only imagine
                        what you're feeling.

                        That also means
                                I'm so proud."

"I'm scared."

                "It's okay to be scared."
                        Steve rubs my back.
                        And I let him.
                                "It's okay."

I'M TIRED OF SECRETS

It feels heavier
    now,

holding this
    secret.

At school, I
    wonder

how long it will be like
    this—

Where I feel like a
    liar
           a
    coward
           a
    fraud—

when I'm none of those,
    right?

"Lev,"
        I say.
        I catch him
                after school.
"I'm freaking out."

        Levi looks at me
        And I think he sees
                the duct tape
                        holding in tears.
                The toothpicks
                        holding up smiles.
                The calm
                        that is the storm.

                "Okay, J,
                        let's go."

                                He finds Evan,
                                        picking his
                                        boyfriend out
                                        of the crowd
                                        without
                                        having to
                                        search for
                                        his red hair.

                                Telling him
                                that he can't
                                go for coffee
                                right now.

Levi drives.

My teeth
          shake in the cold.

My fingers
          shake in the panic.
                    The fear
                              finally allowed
                              out
                              even when the secret is not.

My brain is
          relieved,
                    letting go of its hold
                              on the false face
                              beaten by fear.

                                        Levi looks concerned,
                                                       pulling into
                                                       an empty
                              parking lot. "Talk to me, J."

"I think my mom
          will hate me."

                              "That's not going
                                        to happen."

My brain screams
        out about
        her reaction to his
        coming out.

But even now,
        (even like this)
        I can't tell him.
        Another secret to keep.

                        "Jamie,
                                I need you
                                to

                b r e a t h e

                        for me."

B r e a t h e.

                        "No matter what,
                        Steve has your back,
                                and so do I."

He whispers,

                        "Your family isn't Evan's."

I close my eyes.

I am everything I need to be right now and it's enough.

"I hate this.
    Nothing is happening,
        and I'm a mess."

        Levi laughs,
          "*A lot* is
            happening.
          You always get
          annoyed
          when you have a
            panic attack.

        But, J,
          you're
          allowed to
            panic."

"It was so good
        to figure myself
        out,
        to know who I am.

But the fact that
        I feel like
                I'm lying
                to everyone

        makes me feel
                        like garbage.

And I can't change
        that I am
                        who I am.

But I can change
        that it's a secret.

But I can't control
        the hate people
        may have
for what I am."

Then,
in this car,
        heat finally kicking in,

        Levi tells me,

                "It's okay
                to keep secrets,

                but it's better
                to be yourself."

He remembers.

                "Fear tells you
                you're these things.

                You're not
                doing anything

                wrong."

                He smiles.

                        "For once, Jamie,
                        let it be about you.

                        Tell them
                        when you feel
                        like you're ready,
                        not when you feel
                        like they are."

"THE DAY"

I let weeks
     go by.

        And I am myself

              for myself.

I get to know
     genderqueer Jamie.

The binder Steve buys me
      is great.
          Black and much more
            comfortable.

        Less noticeable if you're looking,
          invisible if you aren't.

I feel good.
I still don't have a plan,
no day feels like The Day
to tell them, but then…

My parents are watching
        the news, and
        there's a kid
        who is trans.

                "I don't understand," Mom says.
                "How could that little girl know?"

                "I'm not sure," my father agrees.
                "It's not a genetic thing."
                Like he would know. Because he's
                a scientist.

Is this how
        they would talk
        about me?
I'm so surprised that now,
        I have to know.

"It doesn't matter
how old you are," I blurt out.

My dad notices
        me shaking, pauses
        the news.

Then I say,
"I need you to support me."

                They say "of course"
                quickly, looking panicked,
                looking surprised.

Here goes:
"I'm genderqueer."

I breathe
     deeply,
     thankful, proud even, that
     it (I) came out
     without fear.

          There's a long pause.

            "Okay, honey,"
            says my father,
            slowly.
            "I think I know what
            that means. But
            can you explain
            so I'm sure?"

I think
     he may be
     lying.

But I also think
     he's doing it
     to make me
     feel okay.

So I explain.

A LITTLE DOES GO A LONG WAY

My parents
  don't really
  understand
  what I am.

But my parents
  understand
  who I am.
  That their kiddo
  is still everything
  that they wanted me to be.

          ("Maybe more,"
            my Dad adds,
            hugging me.)

I'm able to sink safely
    in their arms.
    And I let fear
        turn into tears of gratitude
            and relief.

It takes some time
        for my parents to turn
                "she" into "they,"

                "daughter" into "child" or "kiddo."
                        (Or "spawn" which is what Dad
                        has always joked about anyway.)

                "Gender" into a spectrum.
                        Going from
                                two defined things
                        into something
                                much bigger.

Steve,
        of course,
                answers questions
                they're afraid to ask me

                (mostly about grandchildren).

Mom is slow,
        hates being corrected,
        but she is trying.
                A sigh turns
                        into a
                        question of

                        "How can I do this better?"

Dad learns
        too quickly,
        and I have to tell him
        not to be
"too embarrassing,"

                that

"I still hate attention, Dad"

        when he tries to
        single-handedly
        defeat
        the gender binary.

I'VE NEVER BEEN HAPPIER TO BE WRONG

Levi smiles
      his goofy grin
      when I tell him
      at school.
      Lifts me up,
          laughing.
          Saying, "I told you so"
          over and over again.

And while I'd normally
      be mad at him
      for rubbing it in,

I grin and say,
"You were right.
You were right.
You were right, Lev."

I tell him
      that I want to
      get used to my parents
      knowing

("It's still crazy
      that they know!")

      before I tell
      our friends.

It's not me
      hiding from them.

("Okay, maybe it's me
      hiding a little bit.")

But there are so many
      feelings
      that come with
      coming out.

And this way,
        my parents
        can adapt.

So they don't say
        anything
        offensive
        in front of
        everyone.

But I will, soon.
        I want to soon.

I'm excited for them
        to know me, too.

DOWN BY THE WATER

It's November,
>and we're given
>one more warm weekend.
>A surprise bookended by
>cold fronts. So

it only seems right
>to slip down to
>the water.

Everyone has said that
>I seem different.
>But, of course,
>only Levi knows why.

So, sitting there,
>skipping rocks,

I break our rules.
>I make no announcement
>of a secret.

I say,

"Hey,
          I use they/them pronouns now."

I don't cry or
          let them ask
          any questions.

And it's funny
          to think I was afraid,
          but I know it's normal.

I know I'm normal.
          Well,
          at least,
          this isn't what
          makes me weird...

but my friends knew that
          already.

Jason asks questions.
> Eric gets protective.
> Callie stays quiet.
> Nora smiles as if she knew.
> Levi makes a joke.

Then,
> we go back to
> what we were doing.

Someone suggests
> we order a pizza,
> and we laugh
> at the idea of
> an unlucky delivery person
> > climbing
> > down here.

> > > "I don't think we'd
> > > > ever have enough
> > > > money to tip them
> > > > for that," Jason says.

CATCHING "IT"

The sound of
     a ball in a glove.

The *thwack*,
        a knock
        announcing
        its arrival.

The pinch
     of the glove
     covered by my hand,
     so the ball doesn't fall
              out.

And the decision of
     how to throw
     a secret
     so it leaves
     my hand
        just right.

These things have always
     made me feel
     in control.

So I always ask Steve
     to play catch
     when he comes home.

One of my grandmas
        has decided to
        decide what I am
        (a freak).

And one of our aunts
        has decided to
        agree with her.

        And also
        to not speak
        to me.

Even when I think
        that the ball
                has a better chance
                of hitting me
        than of me
                catching it,

I still try. So I wonder
        why I learned that
        and they didn't.

It's a better use
        of time than
        when I cry
        and wonder
        what's wrong with me
        that they don't
        love me anymore.

I wish I could tell them, with a smile:
        queer isn't contagious.

My parents
    do what
    they think
    is best and

    try to
    shield me
    from a world
    that I've
    always
    known.

    Where
    gender
            is
            everywhere.
    And so

    I play
    the adult
    and

    take the
    fear

    others have
    of me
            and
                    I am stronger

(in the moment).

            I let it take
                its toll later. Then
                        let it go.

178

I wouldn't say
    it's easy
    knowing that

some people
    would demand
    a gender. And that

my driver's license
    will still say
    "F" where

other states
    allow an
    "X." Or that

so many places
    make me choose
    a restroom based on signs.

Gender is still everywhere,
    the most popular pair
    since black and white.

And why must I say that
     "I'm lucky"
     to be accepted
     rather than to say,
     "People need to do better.
     I'm still a person"?

It's easy to be angry.
     But then it's harder to
     be okay
     (even if I'm right)
     because being mad
     is so
     t i r i n g.

(I spent some time practicing
     this anger, and sometimes,
     I still do.)

THE SECOND READING

When I talk about
  the reading,
  it's Nora who
  falls in love
  with the image

of a poet
  speaking
  in a small space.

Of seeing art
  up close,

having never been able to go.
  So Levi watches the twins,
  and I promise she'll be home
  soon.

Selfishly, I find
      another queer poet,
      and they too
      speak so casually
      about binding.

Nora leans over,
      whispers questions
      about it, so

without thinking, I say,
      "Yeah,
      it's really common
      in the community.
      I do it, too."

She nods. Says,
      "Thanks, Jamie."

I get home later,
    slide
    another book of poetry
    next to the first.

I drop into
    the chair,
    panic.

Feel my heart race
    behind my eyes,
    in my chest,
    on my wrists.

Almost text Nora,
    beg her to keep
    this secret. And

then,
    I breathe,
    repeat,
        "It's really common."

I check for feelings
        of shame,
        of fear,
        of regret,

thinking they couldn't
        have passed
        for good. But

for now, at least,
        they're gone,
        and I smile.

I still won't
        tell my parents
        right now.

But that door
        doesn't seem
        shut so tightly.

And I think
        I trust them
                when they say
                "I love you" now.

So "The Day" exists again,
        except it'll just be
        "a day" in my future,
        I hope.

EVERYONE HAS A SECRET IN HIGH SCHOOL

At least, that's what
    my older brother, Steve, says,

    and he's right.

Some girls date boys.
    And even these girls
    sometimes keep this
    from their parents.
    Parents who judge
    boyfriends based
    on race, money,
    things we can't control.

Some girls ask:
    "Hey Mom, Dad,
    can I have a friend
    over to watch Disney movies?"
    But that girl-space-friend isn't
    just a "friend."
    But their parents
    would never say "okay"
    if they knew that.

Some girls play
         spin the bottle,
         around and around it goes,
         but I still don't know.

My friends see movies
and eat ice cream,
         and, according to my mother,
         we're growing.

(I think
she's proud
that we can
talk about
certain things
in a way
she never could.)

I'm pretty sure now
         my parents
         would never believe
         that I was one of
         "those girls."

 Because I'm not.

We have secrets too,
but not all of them
are the same as they
used to be.

Levi's gay.
(He and Evan Holmes
won Homecoming Court
this year, and
Levi's parents were proud of both of them.)

Nora's dad still drinks too much.
(She's thinking about telling
someone though.)

Eric dropped out of swimming.
And his mother has
finally accepted it.

Jason and Callie
tell us
she's not sure she's straight and
he feels like he doesn't have a secret.
(We say "that's okay" to both.)

We still pile into Eric's van,
and drive to the park.

    Climb down
    onto the rocks
    by the canal.
    Off of the trails where

        our parents
        brought us for
        Sunday cookouts.
        Days with
        picture-perfect
        picnic baskets, and
        family Frisbee matches.

We talk about
        our classmates and
        our teachers.
        Complain about
        assignments, tests,
        and quizzes.

        We talk about
        everything. Including
        how good it is to
                be honest with each other.
        And how lucky we are
                to always return here.

One by one,
we have each come

to the canal,
picked a normal weekend outing.

> Held court.
> Called a meeting.
> All of those adult terms.
> And we realize that
> we've all changed so much
> because we've come
> to say to the water
> what scared us most.

We still keep secrets,
    and we still tell our own.

All of us.

But we don't let fear
    decide what's a secret
    and what isn't.

Because it is safety, rather than secrets,
    that binds us together.

WANT TO KEEP READING?

If you liked this book, check out another book

from West 44 Books:

SECOND IN COMMAND BY SANDI VAN

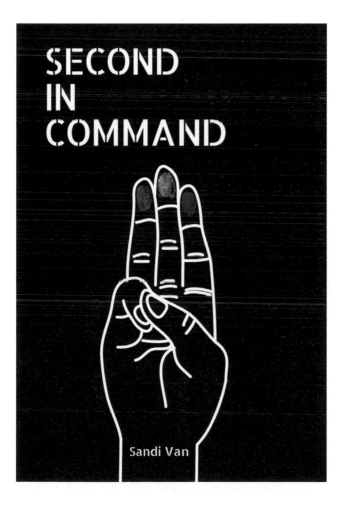

THE DAY MOM LEFT

Early in the morning—
so early
the darkness was a blanket
over my face.

Like when Jack and I
would build a fort in the family room,
hide underneath,
and eat bowls of salty popcorn.

You better clean up those crumbs,
Mom would say.

Today she says,
Goodbye.
I love you.
Take care of Reina,
and Daddy,
and each other.

Six months will go by fast,
I promise.

Then she kisses us each
three times—
once on the left cheek,
once on the right,
once on the forehead,
her lips like wet dough.

Check out more books at:
www.west44books.com

An imprint of Enslow Publishing

WEST **44** BOOKS™

ABOUT the AUTHOR

Rory James is a writer from Cleveland, Ohio. She holds degrees in creative writing, English, and political science. Rory now teaches test prep classes to high school students. Inspired by her own experience with gender issues, Rory hopes to reach the many young people with struggles or questions of their own.